BLOODLINES
EMERGENCY
OPS

written by
M. Zachary Sherman

illustrated by
Raymund Bermudez

coloured by
Raymund Lee

DEDICATED TO THE MEN AND WOMEN
OF THE ARMED FORCES

Raintree is an imprint of Capstone Global Library Limited,
a company incorporated in England and Wales having its
registered office at 7 Pilgrim Street, London, EC4V 6LB -
Registered company number: 6695582

To contact Raintree, please phone 0845 6044371,
fax + 44 (0) 1865 312263,
or email myorders@raintreepublishers.co.uk.

First published by Stone Arch Books © 2012
First published in the United Kingdom in 2013
The moral rights of the proprietor have been asserted.

Editor: Vaarunika Dharmapala
Art Director: Bob Lentz
Graphic Designer: Brann Garvey
Production Specialist: Michelle Biedscheid

ISBN 978 1 406 26192 9 (paperback)
17 16 15 14 13
10 9 8 7 6 5 4 3 2 1

British Library Cataloguing in Publication Data
A full catalogue record for this book is available from the British Library.

CONTENTS

PERSONNEL FILE

Captain
Anne Donovan

ORGANIZATION:
US Army Nurse Corps

ENTERED SERVICE AT:
Camp Pendleton, CA, USA

BORN:
12th December 1946

EQUIPMENT

- dog tags
- military-issue uniform
- first-aid pouch
- .45 calibre pistol
- combat boots

OVERVIEW: VIETNAM WAR

The Vietnam War began as a conflict over what kind of government the country would have: communist or capitalist. At the start of the war in 1959, South Vietnam and North Vietnam were two separate countries. South Vietnam battled the communist Vietcong of the South and the communists of North Vietnam. The Vietcong and North Vietnam wanted to unite the two countries into one communist nation. They were backed by the Soviet Union and China. Under the leadership of President Lyndon Johnson, the United States supported South Vietnam with money and troops.

PRESIDENT JOHNSON

MAP

VIETNAM

Hamburger Hill

THAILAND

LAOS

CAMBODIA

GULF OF
THAILAND

SOUTH
CHINA SEA

MISSION

Captain Anne Donovan heads to the front lines. Along with a small medical unit, she'll provide aid to the soldiers at Hamburger Hill.

CHAPTER 001

HOTEL MEATBALL

FWOOSH! FWOOSH! FWOOSH!

Three Bell UH-1 helicopters swept through the hot, humid air above South Vietnam. The distinct beats of their blades were immediately identifiable, even in the noisy combat zone. Usually, the sound meant salvation to the troops on the ground. In NhaTrang, however, that noise was a sure sign that more wounded soldiers were about to arrive.

The coastal Vietnamese city was home to the US Army's 8th Field Hospital, nicknamed Hotel Meatball. It was a front-line hospital tasked with taking all injured soldiers from the nearby combat zones. Within a series of small personnel tents, dozens of doctors and nurses patched up lightly wounded soldiers and quickly moved them back into the fight. The seriously wounded were prepped for extraction to Japan or Hawaii.

The smells of war hung in the air as the helicopters, hot jet wash oozing from their tail pipes, soared towards the drop zone. On the ground, twenty olive-green-clad men and women rushed from their tents like fire ants from a dirt hill. The overhead PA system blared: "All personnel, hear this! Incoming wounded on the pad!" The voice echoed through the camp, signalling the start of another long day.

The hospital staff sprinted down the lines of tents with emergency medical gear clutched in their hands. Captain Anne Donovan, running up alongside one of the nurses, grinned. "What do you hear from the corpsman underground, Kathy?" she asked.

Together, the women hoofed it over the dusty roads towards the sound of the approaching wounded. RN Kathy Martin furrowed her brow with sadness. "Looks like a squad of Marines were ambushed on patrol," she answered.

Donovan frowned. "You know the drill," she said. "Concentrate on the ones we can save – stabilize them and rush them to post-op."

"And the others?" Nurse Martin asked quietly.

"The others –" Donovan's voice trailed off as the two women spotted the metal chopper skids hit the ground. In an instant, the medical teams swarmed the helos and began unloading the wounded.

Even for a nurse like Captain Donovan, this was a grisly and frightful sight. She had only been in Vietnam for three months. Though she put on a brave face for the other doctors and nurses, seeing these wounded men – these boys – hurt her to her core. She hoped it would never stop being frightening.

The helos had delivered fifteen soldiers, all with life-threatening injuries. The medics first strapped them to stretchers. Then they lined up the wounded in order of those they knew they could save. Those who didn't have much time left got sent to the back of the line.

The soldiers had been ambushed, unaware of what was happening until it was too late. Their injuries showed it. US Army Rangers were regarded as the strongest of all the fighting men, but in this war, the Vietcong had home-field advantage.

Many of the Rangers on board the choppers had AK-47 bullet holes and shrapnel wounds. Others had been unlucky enough to fall into homemade traps. These were holes dug into the ground by the enemy, and then covered with a camouflage netting of trees and twigs that disguised pits of deadly bamboo poles. One Ranger had taken a death trap through the chest. He'd lost a lot of blood, but he wasn't the worst casualty. Many of the boys weren't going to live through the day.

Donovan looked at Martin, whose eyes were welling with tears. "Make them comfortable," she ordered.

Then, kneeling next to one of the wounded US Marines, Captain Donovan smiled. The young man grimaced back at her in pain, his morphine wearing thin. "Are you an angel?" the Marine asked softly with a Southern drawl.

Donovan shook her head. "No, I'm a nurse."

"Oh, thank God," the man replied. "I was afraid you were here to take me away. How's it look?"

Donovan opened the Marine's blood-soaked shirt.

"You're lucky," said Donovan.

And he was. A grenade had exploded next to the soldier. However, the explosive had landed in thick mud, which had safely dispersed the explosion.

"Post-op! Now!" Donovan shouted. "I want this Marine prepped and on the table in five minutes."

Nurse Martin immediately crouched down and opened her field kit. She placed an IV in the soldier's arm and taped the needle down.

Donovan ordered the nurses to haul the injured man out of the area. The nurses lifted the stretcher and rushed him to the surgical tents as quickly as they could.

Running alongside the stretcher, Captain Donovan checked the Marine's vitals. She held his bottle of plasma high above her head. "Don't worry, Sergeant Ford –" she started.

The young man stretched out a bloody hand. He wrapped it around Donovan's arm. "Bobby," he said quietly as the two Army corporals carried him with care down the path.

Captain Donovan looked at the man and grinned. There was something there, an instant spark between them. "Bobby," she repeated. "We'll get you back on your feet in no time, sir."

"I hope not," Sergeant Ford replied. He let out a pained laugh. "You're the best thing I've seen since I landed in this jungle."

"Charmer," said Captain Donovan. Then she took off in a sprint, barking orders as medics neared the operating room tent.

DEBRIEFING

UH-1 HELICOPTER

HISTORY

During the early 1950s, the US Army selected the UH-1 as their medical evacuation helicopter. The twin-pilot, twin-engine vehicles quickly took on a variety of tasks during Vietnam, including transportation and air assaults. More than 7,000 UH-1s served in the conflict, but more than half were destroyed in battle.

SPECIFICATIONS

FIRST FLIGHT: 22nd Oct 1956
ROTOR DIAMETER: 48 feet
LENGTH: 57.3 feet
HEIGHT: 14.9 feet
MAX SPEED: 139.15 mph
RANGE: 197.8 miles
CEILING: 14,200 feet

1 foot = 0.30 metres
1 mile = 1.6 kilometres

FACT

Today, UH-1s are the most widely used military helicopters. They are often known by the nickname, the "Huey".

US ARMY NURSE CORPS

HISTORY

The US Congress created the US Army Nurse Corps, or the NC, in 1901. It is one of six medical Special Corps which make up the Army Medical Department, or AMEDD. The NC is comprised of registered nurses (RNs) who function as medical service providers to government actions and campaigns.

IN VIETNAM

During the Vietnam War, many Army nurses were deployed to South-East Asia, staffing important Army hospitals in the area, including in Saigon, Cam Ranh Bay, and Da Nang. Due to guerrilla warfare tactics used by opposing soldiers, many Army nurses were exposed to, and killed by, enemy fire.

NURSE CORPS MISSION

"All actions and tasks must lead and work toward promoting the wellness of Warriors and their families, supporting the delivery of Warrior and family healthcare, and all those entrusted to our care and ultimately, positioning the Army Nurse Corps as a force multiplier for the future of military medicine."

CHAPTER 002

SCRUBS

Twelve hours. Most nurses at Hotel Meatball could count on spending that much time in surgery each and every day. But when Captain Anne Donovan, her white scrubs stained with the blood of several men, exited the surgical tent, time wasn't on her mind. No, she was focused on something deeper and more painful. She needed to keep the emotions inside, keep them bottled up. If she let them slip out, Donovan knew she'd never seal them up again.

Donovan tried to shake it off, that feeling of dread that was becoming worse with every hour spent in the operating room. Experiencing death was part of her job, but this was different. The things she'd seen in these last few months would stay with her for life. Donovan knew that, but she also knew she was a soldier now, not just a nurse. And those boys needed both.

Never in her life had Donovan imagined this much death. The sight was becoming more than she could bear. The soldiers' wounds weren't accidental mishaps. These were violent injuries. Worse of all, they were intentional. Other men had inflicted this pain on purpose.

Stop thinking like that! Just stop! Donovan told herself as she slowly made her way out of the operating tent. She headed over to the far end of the army camp. *Don't think about it. . .*

The sun was gone, and stars littered the night sky. Captain Donovan walked behind the tent. She removed her cap and threw it on the ground. Slumping down on to a wooden crate, she reached under her uniform and pulled a pack of cigarettes from her pocket.

She searched her pockets for her antique lighter, but she couldn't find it.

"Oh no, where's Grandpa's lighter?" she said. "If I've lost it, I'll –!"

Just then, cast in the glow of the full moon, a long shadow passed over her.

"This what you're looking for?" a voice said. "Those things will kill ya, you know."

Looking up, Donovan saw Dr Brian Woods, an Army colonel, lifetime soldier, and the Chief Medical Officer at the camp. Woods held a brass World War I trench lighter in his hand.

"So will the hours," Donovan joked. She took the lighter, lit her cigarette, and placed it back in her pocket.

A small metal thermos in one hand, Woods moved slowly over to the boxes.

"Find your own crate. This one's taken." Donovan smiled and crumpled the pack of smokes in her hand.

"This was my personal spot before you got here, ma'am. You're trespassing," Woods said, dropping down on to the makeshift wooden seat.

"Guess rank does have its privileges, eh, colonel?" Donovan replied.

"And what kind of nurse smokes, anyway?" Woods asked.

"The tired kind," Donovan answered.

Donovan and Woods took a minute before either said anything. They just sat there, eyes skyward, gazing at the stars.

"How'd your team do today?" Dr Woods finally asked, unscrewing the lid of his thermos.

"Eighty per cent, sir," Captain Donovan said softly.

"Better than me," replied Woods. He sipped at the warm coffee he'd stolen from the mess tent. "I had bullet wounds of all kinds – AK-47s, M1911s, you name it. Heck, one even entered the soldier's leg and bounced around up into his stomach."

"We had one kid, barely twenty," Donovan began. "A pilot. He'd been –" the captain stopped short. Her voice began to crack. Lowering her face, Donovan tried to hold back her emotions.

After a moment, the captain took a deep breath and then continued. "He'd been shot down by a MiG-21," she said. "Ejected safely, but the kid had already been cut up pretty bad by shrapnel. He was bleeding everywhere."

Woods whistled with concern.

"The doc put him back together," Donovan said, "and spent the next four hours pulling pieces of sharpened metal the size of dimes out of his chest cavity."

"But he's going to live, right?" asked Dr Woods.

Captain Donovan nodded.

"Then you did your job," Woods said.

"That's not good enough, sir," Donovan said. She stood, throwing the pack of cigarettes on the ground. "It's like every kid they bring in here, we patch up with spare parts so he'll be good enough to put back on the line. We're not saving lives, we're just delaying the inevitable."

"You see yourself as a healer, is that it?" Woods asked.

Donovan nodded. "Yes, sir."

"Then what are you doing in my army?" Woods asked, glaring up at her.

"I thought I could come here, help Americans –"

"Bull," Woods interrupted. "You could've worked at a VA hospital to do that. Why'd you really come here?"

Captain Donovan waited a moment. Then she looked down at her commanding officer. He took another slow sip from his thermos.

"To prove something –" Donovan began.

"To who?" Woods shot back. "What, Daddy didn't get a son, is that it? You went off to go to war to prove you were worthy of his love?"

"No, sir, Daddy got his son, and he's an F-4 pilot," Donovan replied. "No, I wanted to prove it to myself."

"Prove what?" Dr Woods prodded.

"Prove I actually had what it takes to do this job," said the captain. "I thought if I could come out here, be on the frontier of medicine, on the edge … I could prove I could someday be a doctor."

All at once, the tears came streaming down her face. Wrapping her arms around herself, Captain Donovan stood in the moonlight, sobbing.

Finally, after a moment, Woods rose. His stern, angular face had softened. He placed a hand on Donovan's shoulder and smiled.

"Heckuva place to do a residency, huh?" Woods said. Chuckling, the doctor wiped Donovan's tears away from her cheeks.

"Yes, sir," Donovan answered quietly.

"The fact you're having this kind of reaction to what's going on around here tells me you're going to be a terrific doctor," said Woods. "One of the best I've ever seen, Donovan. But you're no soldier."

Slowly, she looked up at him. "What?"

"We're not healers here, we're mechanics," said Woods. "It's our job to keep the machinery running, day in and day out. Slap spare parts on them and get them back into the fight. You look at these kids as people with families, girlfriends, mothers. . ."

Woods shook his head and paused for a moment.

"You can't," he said. "Bedside manners have no place in a combat zone. We get these boys back on to the line so they can fight the good fight. We're assemblymen fixing a war machine – and they're the cogs."

"That's horrible!" Donovan exclaimed.

"I know," Dr Woods said. "But that's the way it is. After you get them walking, *then* show some compassion. Until then? It's your skills as a nurse they need, not your compassion. Can you do that, Captain?"

Donovan nodded. "How do you do it, day in, day out around here?" she asked.

"I'm a soldier, and a doctor," Woods answered. "It's my job."

Colonel Woods picked up his thermos, screwed the top back on, and turned to go. "Tomorrow, I'm pulling you from duty, Captain," he said. "I want you to take some time out of the operating room."

"But Major –" started Donovan.

"No buts, Captain," said Woods sternly. "For the next two weeks, I want you to do your rounds, and then when you feel up to it, I want you to go to the village on the MEDCAP. Understood?"

"Yes, sir," said Captain Donovan.

"Fine. Now –" Woods waved at the pack of cigarettes on the ground. "Put those in the bin," he said. "I won't accept littering in my post," he said.

With that, Colonel Woods walked back into the operating tent, leaving Donovan alone with her last cigarette and her thoughts.

WEAPONS OF WAR

MiG-21

FIRST FLIGHT: 14th Feb 1955
WING SPAN: 23 feet, 6 inches
LENGTH: 51 feet, 9 inches
HEIGHT: 15 feet, 9 inches
WEIGHT: 18,080 lbs.
MAX SPEED: 1,300 mph
RANGE: 400 miles
CEILING: 50,000 feet
CREW: One

1 foot = 0.30 metres
1 inch = 2.54 centimetres
1 pound = 0.45 kilograms
1 mile = 1.6 kilometres

HISTORY

Designed by the Mikoyan-Gurevich Design Bureau in the Soviet Union, the MiG-21 is the most produced supersonic jet aircraft in aviation history. The first MiG-21s arrived in North Vietnam from the Soviet Union by ship in April 1966. The aircraft did not have the long-range radar and missiles that the US fighter planes had. However, the MiG-21 was a deadly threat in high-speed, hit-and-run attacks. This combat success led the US Air Force and US Navy to develop fighter training schools to improve the defence against these types of attacks.

WEAPONS OF WAR

SAM MISSILES

As early as the Civil War (1861–1865), nations searched for ways to protect themselves from aerial attacks. During WWI and WWII, this defence often came in the form of mounted anti-aircraft guns. Soon, however, quicker and higher-flying aircraft became more difficult to defend against. In the mid-1940s, Germany developed the first guided surface-to-air missile (SAM) called the Wasserfall. Many countries, including the US, developed their own SAM. By the Vietnam War, these weapons became the standard.

FACTS

– The first surface-to-air missiles in the Vietnam War were fired on 25th July 1965. The missiles struck four US F-4 fighters, taking down one and damaging three.

– The SA-2 surface-to-air missile, popular during the Vietnam War, could shoot 60,000 feet into the air and travel at more than 2,500 miles per hour.

– Surface-to-air missiles are also know as ground-to-air missiles (GTAM).

CHAPTER 003

AN ANGEL

The post-operation tent was quiet as a tomb, filled with eighteen men resting after surgery. All of the post-op beds were in two lines, their headboards placed against the walls. There were ten beds on each side, creating an aisle between them.

At the foot of each patient's bed was a small metal clipboard hanging from a metal loop. These were medical charts that listed each patient's vital statistics for the supervising nurses to review each hour.

Captain Donovan walked down the aisle surveying her patients. She looked over when she heard a familiar voice from behind her.

"Hey, Angel!" the man said.

Smiling broadly, she ducked her head so the speaker couldn't see her expression. She composed herself, and then turned around.

"Sergeant Ford," she said, walking over to the foot of his bed. She took his chart and examined it.

"Bobby, remember?" he said, a sly grin on his face.

"Yes, I remember," she answered. "Your vitals look pretty good, Bobby."

"Thanks to you, Angel," said the soldier.

"Well, you just get better so we can get you outta here, okay?" Donovan said.

Ford's grin vanished. "Wait, I'm not going home, am I?" he said anxiously.

Walking over to his bedside, Captain Donovan sat down in a small wooden chair. She leant over to him, placing her hand on his wrist and checking his pulse.

"Nope, you're going to be just fine in about two weeks. Back in the saddle with your unit," Donovan said as she timed his heartbeats with her watch.

"You scared me," said Ford. "I couldn't imagine leaving my boys behind. Most of them are too young to shave, let alone be Rangers."

Ford paused. "I need to help 'em along, you know?"

Donovan smiled at this. She had felt the same way about some of the men that had passed through her care.

"Back in the saddle, eh?" Ford said. "Where you from anyway?"

Clutching the clipboard to her chest, Captain Donovan looked up and brushed the hair away from her eyes. "My family's originally from Illinois, but I grew up in Cheyenne, Wyoming," she said.

"I knew it!" exclaimed Ford. "I'm from Laramie, Texas. I knew I heard a twang in your voice." He tried to sit up, but stopped at the first sign of pain in his chest.

Donovan placed a consoling hand on his shoulder. "The twang only comes out when I'm angry," she said. "So easy there, Ranger, or you'll get to hear more of it."

"I hope so." Ford smiled as he lay back down.

Donovan walked over and replaced his chart at the foot of his bed. "You get some rest," said the captain. "And be more careful next time, will ya?"

"Not a chance," he said, struggling into a sitting position despite the obvious pain. "It's the only way I'll get to see you again, Angel."

Shaking her head, Captain Donovan turned to go. Then she narrowed her eyes, turned back to him, and smiled. "Look me up after the war, GI," she said softly. "You know where I live."

Ford beamed. "Count on it, Angel," he said.

DEBRIEFING

WEAPONS OF WAR

AK-47 RIFLE

SERVICE: 1949–present
DESIGNER: Mikhail Kalashnikov
WEIGHT: 9.5 pounds
LENGTH: 34.3 inches with fixed
wooden stock; 34.4 inches with
folding stock extended; 25.4 inches
with stock folded
BARREL: 16.3 inches
RATE OF FIRE: 600 rounds/min.
EFFECTIVE RANGE: 330 yd, full
automatic; 440 yd, semi-automatic

1 pound = 0.45 kilograms
1 inch = 2.54 centimetres
1 yard = 0.9 metres

HISTORY

The AK-47 was first developed in
the Soviet Union. It was one of
the first true assault rifles, and it
continues to be a widely used rifle
today. It remains popular because
it has a low production cost, is
easy to use, and is very durable. It
can be fired as a semi-automatic
or full-automatic rifle. In semi-
automatic mode, it fires only
once when the trigger is pulled.
In full-automatic mode, the rifle
continues to fire until the rounds
are gone or until the trigger is
released. A versatile weapon,
more AK-47s have been produced
than all other assault weapons
combined.

M1911 PISTOL

SERVICE: 1911-present
DESIGNER: John M. Browning
WEIGHT: 2.44 pounds
LENGTH: 8.25 inches
BARREL: 5.03 inches
HISTORY: First used by the US
Army on 29th March 1911, the
M1911 pistol quickly became a
popular weapon for all branches of
the US military. The single-action,
semi-automatic handgun fired .45
calibre cartridges from a seven-
round magazine. During WWII,
the US government purchased
1.9 million M1911s. They remained
a vital weapon throughout the
Vietnam War.

NEW WARFARE

Although handguns remained
a soldier's "best friend", the
US military's reliance on
short-range weapons and
close quarters combat (CQC)
decreased after WWII. Pistols
and hand grenades helped
troops secure combat zones and
protect themselves in enemy-
occupied areas. During Vietnam,
the military often relied on
aerial bombers and precision
weapons to complete these
types of tasks.

CHAPTER 004

THE MISSION

The weeks ran on, and Captain Donovan was starting to feel more at ease with herself and her assignment. Though she'd never admit it, the colonel had been right to take her off the surgery rotation and put her on post-op watch. Helping with the recovery of the men, not facing every hour of the day with another trauma, allowed her to focus and take note of what she'd need to do to survive.

The MEDCAPs didn't hurt her situation either.

Since the United States was technically in Vietnam to stop the spread of communism and oppression and help the local people, the US Army periodically sent doctors and nurses out on Medical Civil Action Programme operations. The MEDCAP doctors and nurses delivered much needed medical supplies, vaccines, and assistance to the local people of Vietnam.

Captain Donovan and Nurse Martin, were scheduled on MEDCAP missions in the area near Phan Rang. With fellow doctors and nurses, they'd dispense medicines to the locals and set up public health programmes. This included treating the sick and providing entire villages with anti-malaria medication, topical creams for a variety of skin conditions, and other antibiotics.

Tucked inside a village chief's hut, Donovan and Martin received a long line of children, varying in age and gender. Donovan sat at a small table, marking off information on several charts and lists as Martin gave shots to the children.

"Come on, dear," Martin said as one of the little girls refused to sit down, a frown pursed upon her lips. Every time Martin came close to her with the hypodermic needle, the little girl backed away. Frustrated, Martin slammed the syringe on the table.

"What's the matter, Martin?" asked Donovan.

"She won't let me give her the shot," Martin said angrily.

Captain Donovan crouched down next to the little girl and smiled at her. "You don't want the shot?" she asked.

The little girl shook her head and frowned.

"But you want to feel better, don't you?" Donovan asked.

The little girl nodded. Captain Donovan casually reached over and picked up the syringe. "Listen, if you don't get the shot, you're not going to be able to grow up big and strong, okay?" she told the little girl. "And you want that, right?"

The girl hesitated, and then nodded.

"Then show me what a big girl you are, okay?" Donovan said. She rolled up the little girl's sleeve and took hold of the child's arm.

Eyes closed tight, the little girl waited in anticipation. To Donovan's surprise, the girl didn't even flinch when Donovan pushed the needle in.

"Not so bad, huh?" Donovan said as she wiped the girl's arm with an alcohol swab. "Sometimes, the things we don't know scare us more than the things we do."

Standing on her tiptoes, the little girl kissed Donovan on the cheek and then bounced off and out of the hut.

"Let's take a break, okay?" Donovan said. Martin nodded eagerly.

"You're really good with them, ma'am. The kids, I mean," Martin said. She and Donovan strode along a path. They passed by the small huts that made up the main part of the village.

Captain Donovan shrugged. Then she looked over at the small, dark-haired heads throughout the village. "They just deserve a chance to be kids, you know?" Donovan said.

Martin looked at the silver captain's bars on Donovan's collar. "That's why you became a nurse," she said.

Nodding, Donovan looked at Martin. She cocked her head to the side. "That, and the long hours," she said. "Nothing like staying up all night on a school night."

"And why'd you join the Army, ma'am?" Nurse Martin asked.

"College, mostly," Martin said. "Do a stint in the Army Reserve, and they pay for me to go to medical school. Who knew a war would break out?"

Donovan let out a nervous laugh. "And how about you?" she asked Martin.

"I wanted to see the world, get out of Podunk, Indiana. Make something of myself," Martin said as she looked around her. "I didn't know I was going to be in a MASH unit, though. I thought I'd be in the green zone, helping the wounded there."

"We've been pretty lucky," Donovan said. "According to the major, some of the hospitals have been coming under fire, sappers and snipers trying to pick off the chopper pilots and doctors on the pads."

Donovan looked into the jungle. "I wouldn't be surprised if we're in some sniper's crosshairs right now."

"Don't say that!" Nurse Martin said, angrily waving her finger at Donovan.

Smiling, Donovan shrugged. "Sorry about that," she said. "Bad joke."

"All due respect, ma'am," replied Martin. "I don't understand how you can be such a softy on the inside but outwardly ... callous."

A look of shock spread over Donovan's face as she stopped and stared at Martin. "Is that what you think of me?" Donovan asked. "That I'm just hard?"

Frowning, Martin shook her head. "Well, no," she said. "But you do make some off-hand comments sometimes. To hide the fact you're scared, just like the rest of us."

"I see," Donovan said softly.

She'd never thought of herself in that way, so this came as a huge surprise. Even during her residency at Laramie County Hospital, Donovan had always been the one who treated people equally and respectfully.

"Like the time Nurse Rose wasn't sure about the dosage of aspirin to give a soldier," Martin said. "And you told her to throw some in his mouth, and whatever landed in there was the right dosage."

Donovan chuckled.

"Yeah, I can see how she might have misconstrued that," she said, grinning.

"Or the time –" Nurse Martin began.

"Okay, okay!" Donovan said, raising her hands. "I get it! I'll try not to take it out on other people, okay?"

"Yes, ma'am," Martin answered.

"Let's get back," Donovan said. "It's going to get dark soon, and the last thing I want to be is out here at night without a full MP escort."

*   *   *

It was several more hours before the medical teams made it back from the MEDCAP. Expecting evening chow, they drove the jeeps into the camp but instead of a line at the mess tent, what Donovan and the others saw made their blood run cold.

The sun was setting, turning the sky an amazing shade of orange, but it was a backdrop to the chaos in the camp. A frenzy of medical personnel rushed from one tent to another.

They fetched supplies as quickly as their feet could carry them. All of the personnel tents were empty, and the lights in the surgical tent, which at this time were usually dark, shone through the front flap.

Jumping out of the truck, Donovan grabbed her bag and rushed to the OR. Nurse Martin was close on her heels.

Nurses were shouting to corpsmen and other soldiers as they made their way through the crowds. "What's going on?" Martin yelled

"I don't know," a nurse replied.

All at once, Donovan spotted a young man and grabbed his arm, stopping him in mid-stride.

"Corporal Vetter, what the heck's going on?" she asked desperately.

Vetter was panting hard, trying to catch his breath. "Army's trying to take Hill 937 again," he finally blurted out.

Donovan rolled her eyes and swore under her breath.

"Hamburger Hill?" Martin asked.

Donovan nodded sternly. "It's been five days! When are they going to give it up?! There isn't any strategic value to –"

"All the wounded are coming straight here," Vetter said breathlessly, "and it's a total mess! And we're running out of everything – gauze, swabs – heck, even the plasma's running low. And now we're down one surgeon."

"Wait, slow down. What are you talking about?" Donovan asked.

"The aid station," Vetter said. "They set up an aid station near the front so they could patch up the light casualties and get 'em back on the line ASAP, but their doc was killed. They need a new doc there pronto."

"We're short-handed," Donovan said, shaking her head. "Who's Woods sending?"

"Himself, ma'am," Vetter said. "Major Woods is going out there personally."

"With who?" Donovan asked.

"No one. He's going alone."

DEBRIEFING

VIETCONG SOLDIERS

BACKGROUND

The Vietcong were people in South Vietnam who supported communism. They fought alongside the North Vietnam military to reunite the two countries into one. These soldiers were trained and supported by North Vietnam's government. Most of the Vietcong were young teens. Many believed in the communist cause. Others had been shamed into joining. Women also took up the Vietcong cause and trained and fought with the men.

COMBAT STYLE

The Vietcong were guerrillas. Guerrillas are not part of a regular army. They often use surprise attacks against their enemies. American soldiers were trained to fight on an open battlefield with tanks, artillery, and warplanes. The Vietcong lacked this expensive equipment. Instead, they surprised their enemies with mortar and gun attacks. They also planted mines along the jungle trails. When the Americans searched through the jungles, many were killed by mines. This style of war was not as familiar to American soldiers and led to high casualties.

CIVILIAN LIFE

CIVILIANS

The Vietcong often lived with the residents of small villages. Some South Vietnamese citizens supported the Vietcong. They helped the guerrillas. Villagers sometimes hid weapons for the Vietcong, and they often refused to answer questions about the guerrillas. Other civilians did not agree with the Vietcong cause, but they helped because they were afraid they would be killed if they did not show their support. Because the Vietcong lived so closely with the civilians, US soldiers could often not tell who were friends and who were enemies.

STATISTICS

The Vietnam War claimed millions of victims. Exact casualty figures are unavailable, but below are official estimates:

GROUP	TOTAL DEATHS
US Military	58,000
S. Vietnam Military	266,000
N. Vietnam Military	849,000
Vietcong	251,000
Civilians	2,000,000

CHAPTER 005

HAMBURGER HILL

After tossing his medical bag into the back seat of a jeep, Major Woods ran over and pushed open the door to the motor pool. Suddenly, he looked up to find Donovan staring him in the face.

"I'll ride shotgun," she said.

"Absolutely not!" Woods shouted. "This is the deepest mess these soldiers have been in yet, and I can't have anyone breaking down on me out there. Donovan, this is the frontline in the bloodiest skirmish to date. There's a chance even I won't make it back!"

"Sir, you know the book better than anyone," Donovan said. "You can't go all John Wayne out there by yourself. You have to take –"

Woods raised a hand, waving her off. "Screw the book! Those boys are getting slaughtered, and they need help now!"

"And so do you!" Donovan said. "You can't go without a nurse to assist you, and you said it yourself. I'm the best one you've got. Let me help you!"

The more they argued, the more likely it was that men were dying. But Woods knew she was right. He could use a second set of hands.

"Fine," Woods finally said.

They loaded into the jeep and he started the engine.

"But if I see one tear, you're outta there," Woods said.

"Then don't get all childish on me," Donovan said, "and control your emotions, sir."

Grinning at her, Woods slammed the shifter into first gear and rocketed out of the motor pool.

*   *   *

In the heat of the mountains of South Vietnam, in the western A Shau Valley, one peak rose high above the jungles – Ap Bia Mountain. The mountainside overshadowed the valley, towering at over three thousand feet.

Ridge upon ridge reached up from the thick forests towards the peak. Trails wound up the sides through the dense bamboo groves and tall elephant grass. In some places, the vegetation was so high that even the soldiers riding in personnel carriers could not see above the pale, silky grass.

Ap Bia was known to the locals as "the mountain of the crouching beast". The Army called it Hill 937. Soldiers nicknamed it Hamburger Hill.

Night had fallen before Woods and Donovan arrived, and already the sky was lit up like the Fourth of July. Rockets soared through the air, muzzle flashes lit up hot-spots in the trees, and illumination flares glided down on parachutes like falling stars.

For the past six days, hundreds of soldiers from the US Infantry had been swarming this hill like angry ants, doing everything in their power to capture its hulking mass from the clutches of the North Vietnamese.

But they had failed. And they continued to fail, and fail hard.

The 7th and 8th Battalions of the enemy's 29th PAVN Regiment had successfully kept the Americans at bay. Still, the US Air Force had been pummelling the mountaintop for days, deploying thousands of pounds of ordnance, including the deadly chemical napalm.

With over thirty-five Americans dead and at least one hundred wounded, something had to change to ensure their success. But tactics came from a different part of the Army than Captain Anne Donovan and Major Woods were familiar with. None of that mattered to them as they stood in a small tent a mere kilometre from the majority of the fighting. Here, with limited support from the combat medics, they spent the next eleven hours on their feet, operating on the wounded.

One after another the soldiers came, with injuries ranging from missing limbs to massive skull wounds and everything in between. Only some of the wounded could be saved. For the rest, Donovan and Woods tried to make their passing as comfortable as possible.

It wasn't easy.

The smell of cordite wafted through the air from nearby explosions. The doctors had to yell at one another over concussive blasts that shook the ground around them.

Though the treatment space was smaller than their OR, each doctor navigated the clutter well. Still, only the most rudimentary tools were at their disposal. The innards of a medic's kit sprawled over a small table. Scalpels and forceps swam in an alcohol and blood mixture on a small metal tray. A battery-powered ventilator chugged on the floor beneath them, and a small suction machine hissed in the darkness.

It was crude and gruesome, but somehow, they still managed to save lives.

The floor was littered with filth. Cleanliness wasn't their major concern here. Used sponges and bloody gauze sat crumpled on the wooded planks. In the back, a small post-op was set up with a team of medics doing the finishing work. The surgeons needed to concentrate on the more difficult and life-threatening procedures.

On either side of a small surgical table in the centre of the room, Woods and Donovan worked diligently. They were doing their best to save the young man in front of them.

Blood ran from a small hole in his leg, and though they had sewn the femoral artery back together, the wound was still pumping red, sticky liquid on to the floor.

"I need suction!" Woods yelled.

Just as Donovan turned on the suction device, a mortar blew off next to the tent. Dirt and debris flew in through the tent flaps. Donovan leapt on to the soldier's body, protecting the open wound from contamination.

"One more like that, and we might as well give it up," Woods said.

With a pair of forceps, he dug deeper into the man's leg. "Got it," he exclaimed, slowly removing the lead slug from the man's thigh. "Time to close him up!"

Another soldier came over, took the patient off the table, and carried him to another part of the tent. There, his wound would be stitched back together.

"Next!" Donovan yelled. She pulled her surgical mask away from her face. Then she looked over at Major Woods, shaking her head.

"How many's that?" she asked tiredly.

"I lost count at fifteen," Woods admitted.

Suddenly, two soldiers came running in, an unconscious GI carried between them. Blood coated his uniform and his helmet was slung low, shrouding his blackened face from view.

"What've we got, Corporal?" asked Donovan.

"He's been shot up pretty bad," one of the soldiers said. "And the flyboys dropped a load of napalm. Looks like he was caught on the edge of it. We just found him on the hill. He's barely breathing." The soldiers angled the wounded man towards the empty table.

Donovan cleared the last patient's debris and made hasty work cleaning the area.

"Get him on the table," she said as the corporals did their best to set him down softly.

"Get his helmet off," Woods ordered.

The medics reached over and unclasped the chinstrap. The steel pot fell away from the dying man's head, finally revealing his face for the first time.

"Okay, let's –" Donovan stopped as she looked down. She had recognized the injured soldier.

"Hey, Angel," Sergeant Ford whispered. His jaw had been broken in several places from multiple bullet impacts to the face.

Donovan went into shock. Her muscles seized. She was unable to move. Her crystal blue eyes searched for a glimpse of what was once his proud, strong face.

"I –" she tried to speak, but words wouldn't come.

Ford tried to smile, but his cheek muscles didn't work. He was dying and everyone – especially Donovan – knew it. He had only a few minutes left to live.

Major Woods slipped an entire syringe of morphine into Ford's arm, allowing the warm fluid to ease the sergeant's pain. It was the only thing he could do for him.

All Donovan could do was to hold Sergeant Ford's hand in hers.

Ford tried his best to speak. "Don't –" he forced out. It was so soft that Donovan needed to lean down, her ear to his mouth, to make out the rest of his words.

"Don't ... cry ... angel. . ." he whispered. "Least I got to ... see you again. I'll be waiting for you. But ... don't meet me too quickly ... okay?"

Donovan placed her gloved hand against his charred face, cradling it in her palm. "Okay, Bobby," she said softly, fighting hard to keep back her tears, to be strong for him.

For a moment, the sounds of the war – the explosions, the screams, the gunfire – seemed to disappear. Donovan watched Bobby Ford close his eyes and slip silently away, his body going soft and limp, his head slumping into her waiting hand.

And then, he was gone.

Woods slowly placed a white sheet over the sergeant's body and motioned to the corporals to take him away.

"Do you want to go back?" Woods said quietly, turning to Donovan. But she raised her hand and placed her surgical mask back over her face.

Taking a deep breath, Donovan turned to the doorway. She looked out. "Next!" she yelled.

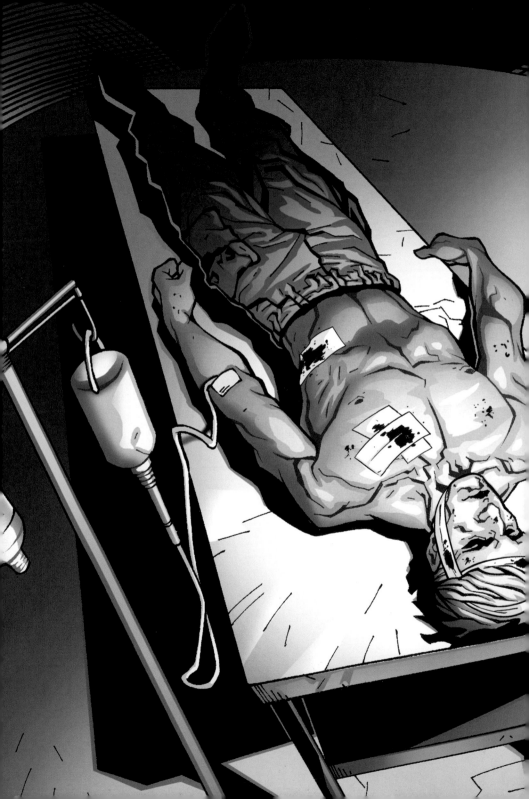

DEBRIEFING

Hamburger Hill

HISTORY

The Battle of Hamburger Hill took place at the Ap Bia Mountain in South Vietnam in 1969, lasting from 10th to 20th May. United States forces and South Vietnamese soldiers fought against North Vietnamese forces in an attempt to take control of Hill 937. US troops moved up the steep hill while battling entrenched North Vietnamese troops. Bad weather, friendly fire, and the North Vietnamese defences made the campaign especially gruelling, but the Airborne troops eventually took the hill through direct assault. The location was nicknamed "Hamburger Hill" for the heavy death tolls incurred by both sides during the conflict.

THE AFTERMATH

In total, the campaign involved the use of ten batteries of artillery, 450 tons of bombs, and 69 tons of napalm by US forces. Reports indicate US losses during the ten-day battle were 72 dead and 372 wounded. Estimates indicate that 630 North Vietnamese soldiers lost their lives during the conflict.

CONTROVERSY

Hill 937 had little strategic value for either side of the war. However, US forces launched a frontal assault to capture it - incurring heavy losses in the process - only to abandon it soon after securing it from the North Vietnamese. The event caused much controversy in the United States for the loss of life and lack of strategic value in fighting for control of the hill.

Vietnam Veterans Memorial

The Vietnam Veterans Memorial is a national memorial in Washington, DC. It remembers and honours US veterans who fought, died, or went missing in the Vietnam War. The memorial has three separate sections: the Vietnam Women's Memorial, the Three Soldiers statue, and the Vietnam Veterans Memorial Wall.

MEMORIAL WALL

The best-known part of the memorial was designed by Maya Lin, and is made of two 246.75-foot-long walls. The apex of the walls, where the two meet, is 10 feet tall, and they taper to a height of eight inches at their ends. Stone for the wall was chosen for its mirror-like appearance. A visitor's reflection can be seen overlapping the names engraved into the walls of the servicemen who were KIA (Killed in Action) or MIA (Missing in Action) in the Vietnam war. One wall points at the Washington Monument, and the other points in the direction of the Lincoln Memorial. The wall lists 58,272 names, including eight women.

THE WOMEN'S MEMORIAL

The Vietnam Women's memorial is south of the Wall. It was dedicated on 11th November 1993, to the women of the United States who served in the Vietnam War. The woman gazing upwards is named Hope, the woman kneeling is named Faith, and the woman healing a wounded soldier is named Charity.

THE THREE SOLDIERS STATUE

Near the wall is a bronze statue of The Three Soldiers. The statue was dedicated in 1984 and shows three soldiers of different ethnicities. The soldiers seem to be looking on in solemn tribute at the memorial wall and the names of their fallen comrades.

ACCLAIM

In 2007, The Vietnam Veterans Memorial was ranked tenth by the American Institute of Architects on their List of "America's Favourite Architecture".

EPILOGUE

Twelve days had passed since the battle of Hill 937.

By day ten of the assault, eighteen hundred men from five infantry battalions of the 101st Airborne – along with ten batteries of heavy artillery, 270 sorties flown by the Air Force, more than 450 tons of ordnance and more than 60 tons of napalm – led the US troops to finally capture the hill.

Though the mission was officially a success, the mainstream media reported it differently: more than three hundred American soldiers were wounded, and seventy-two were killed in action. Civilians at home pondered the relevance of this action, and the cost of the massive mountain in the middle of the jungle was weighed against the value of American lives.

The mountain lost.

Americans were already unhappy with the US presence in Vietnam. But now, things grew steadily worse.

The anger and confusion of people back home began to trickle down to those serving in the war. Many soldiers in-country became unmotivated to fight. Even commanding officers were finding it hard to blindly follow orders from Washington.

But back at Camp Meatball, nothing changed. They still treated the injured and patched men up as best they could – only now Captain Anne Donovan finally understood her role in Vietnam.

The motor pool had been made into a staging area for the long, cold metal boxes that contained the remains of fallen soldiers. Here, they waited until they could be laid to rest on American soil.

And here, among the rows of the dead, Anne Donovan found the coffin of Sergeant Bobby Ford.

Donovan placed a hand on the top of the box. Her body shuddered at the feeling of the cool aluminium casket.

"Such a cold place for such a vibrant man," she whispered.

"Donovan?" a voice called from the door.

Turning, Donovan saw Major Woods enter the room, his cover clutched in his hands. "I read the letter you wrote to Ford's mother. It was beautiful," he said.

She turned away from the coffin and faced her commanding officer. "I wanted to thank you, sir," she said.

"For what, Captain?" Ford said.

"For teaching me why it's important to be a bit distant in what we do," Donovan said. "Teaching me how to be strong. Not just for myself, but mostly –"

Her gaze drifted over the metal boxes sitting motionless in the darkness. She finished, "– so I can be strong for them."

Major Woods nodded. He looked around the massive holding area at the hundreds of boxes waiting to be shipped back to the United States.

"Well," he said, "as long as we're passing out thank yous, guess I owe you one as well."

"Me? What for, sir?" Donovan asked.

"For reminding me that even though I'm a major, I'm a human being first. And not the other way around."

Donovan nodded at her commanding officer.

The blaring sound of the PA system burst out into the darkness: "Attention! Attention! All personnel, incoming wounded on the pads!"

Looking back at Woods, Donovan smiled. "After you, Doctor."

Shaking his head, Major Woods waved his hand at the door. "Ladies first, Captain."

Donovan looked him square in the eye. "I'm no lady," she said. "I'm a soldier. Come on."

She led him out into the night, alive with the hum of helicopters.

EXTRAS

ABOUT THE AUTHOR

M. ZACHARY SHERMAN is a veteran of the United States Marine Corps. He has written comics for Marvel, Radical, Image, and Dark Horse. His recent work includes *America's Army: The Graphic Novel*, *Earp: Saint for Sinners*, and the second book in the SOCOM: SEAL Team Seven trilogy.

AUTHOR Q&A

Q: Any relation to the Civil War Union General William Tecumseh Sherman?

A: Yes, indeed! I was one of the only members of my family lineage to not have some kind of active duty military participation – until I joined the US Marines at age 28.

Q: Why did you decide to join the US Marine Corps? How did the experience change you?

A: I had been working at the same job for a while when I thought I needed to start giving back. The biggest change for me was the ability to see something greater than myself; I got a real sense of the world going on outside of just my immediate, selfish surroundings. The Marines helped me to grow up a lot. They taught me the focus and discipline that helped get me where I am today.

Q: When did you decide to become a writer?

A: I've been writing all my life, but the first professional gig I ever had was a screenplay for Illya Salkind (*Superman* 1-3) back in 1995. But it was a secondary profession, with small assignments here and there, and it wasn't until around 2005 that I began to get serious.

Q: Has your military experience affected your writing?

A: Absolutely, especially the discipline I have obtained. Time management is key when working on projects, so you must be able to govern yourself. In regards to story, I've met and been with many different people, which enabled me to become a better storyteller through character.

Q: Describe your approach to the *Bloodlines* series. Did personal experiences in the military influence the stories?

A: Yes and no. I didn't have these types of experiences in the military, but the characters are based on real people I've encountered. And those scenarios are all real, just the characters we follow have been inserted into the timelines. I wanted the stories to fit into real history, real battles, but have characters we may not have heard of be the focus of those stories. I've tried to retell the truth of the battle with a small change in the players.

Q: Any future plans for the *Bloodlines* series?

A: There are so many battles through history that people don't know about. If they hadn't happened, the world would be a much different place! It's important to hear about these events. If we can learn from history, we can side-step the mistakes we've made as we move forward.

Q: What's your favourite book? Favourite movie? Favourite video game?

A: My favourite book is *The Maltese Falcon* by Dashiell Hammett; I love a good mystery with hard-boiled detectives! As for movie, hands-down it's *Raiders of the Lost Ark*. It is a fantastic story of humanity winning out over evil and the characters are real people thrown into impossible odds. Lots of fun! As for games, there are waaaay to many to mention, but I love sci-fi shooters and first person games.

ABOUT THE ILLUSTRATORS

Raymund Bermudez was born and raised in Quezon City, Philippines. After studying architecture for a couple years, he took up fine arts at the University of the Philippines, focusing on illustration. Since 1998, he's worked on a variety of projects as a freelance illustrator.

Raymund Lee is a comic book colourist based in Manila, Philippines. He got his first break working on the popular Stone and Aria comics. Eventually, he conquered the pages of Marvel comics, including Wolverine, the Uncanny X-Men, and other top titles. His colouring style varies depending on the artwork. A big movie fan, this veteran colourist treats every page or panel as if taken from a movie scene. When not working, he enjoys spending time with his family and two dogs.

THE PROCESS

A CALL TO ACTION

WORLD WAR II

BLOODLINES
DEPTH CHARGE

★ WORLD WAR II ★

M. ZACHARY SHERMAN

KOREAN WAR

BLOODLINES
DAMAGE CONTROL

★ KOREAN WAR ★

M. ZACHARY SHERMAN

During World War II, British Intelligence discovers a German U-505 submarine anchored off the coast of Denmark. Stashed on-board are invaluable codebooks, keys to deciphering the enemy's communications. To secure the documents, a British commando and US Army First Lieutenant Aaron Donovan must team up, sneak aboard the enemy submarine, and get off alive!

During the Korean War, a US Army cargo plane crashes behind enemy lines, and soldiers of the 249th Engineer Battalion are stranded. Facing a brutal environment and attacks by enemy forces, Private First Class Tony Donovan takes action. With spare parts and ingenuity, he plans to repair a vehicle from the wreckage and transport his comrades to safety.

VIETNAM WAR

BLOODLINES
EMERGENCY OPS

VIETNAM ★ WAR ★

M. ZACHARY SHERMAN

IRAQ WAR

BLOODLINES
HEART OF THE ENEMY

IRAQ ★ WAR ★

M. ZACHARY SHERMAN

During the Vietnam War, Captain Anne Donovan of the US Army Nurse Corps heads to the front lines. Along with a small medical unit, she'll provide aid to the soldiers at Hamburger Hill. When the battle intensifies and the deaths multiply, this talented rookie nurse must try to reconcile her role as a healer with the never-ending blood bath that is war.

During the war in Iraq, Lieutenant Commander Lester Donovan of the US Navy SEALs must capture a known terrorist near the border of Syria. It's a dangerous mission. Land mines and hostile combatants blanket the area, yet Donovan is undeterred. But when the mission goes awry, this gung-ho commander must learn to keep his cool, if he's going to keep his men alive.

BLOODLINES